# Danny Dreadnought Saves the World

JONATHAN EMMETT

and

M RTI  L  TI E TO

For Eric
J.E.

To Danny Dreadnought
M.C.

## EGMONT
We bring stories to life

## Book Band: Purple

First published in Great Britain 2014
by Egmont UK Limited
The Yellow Building, 1 Nicholas Road
London, W11 4AN
Text copyright © Jonathan Emmett 2014
Illustrations copyright © Martin Chatterton 2014
The author and illustrator have asserted their moral rights.
ISBN 978 1 4052 7072 4
10 9 8 7 6 5 4 3 2 1
A CIP catalogue record for this title is available from the British Library.
Printed in Singapore.
57032/1

Please note: Any website addresses listed in this book are correct at the time of going to print. However,
Egmont cannot take responsibility for any third party content or advertising. Please be aware that online
content can be subject to change and websites can contain content that is unsuitable for children. We
advise that all children are supervised when using the internet

# Danny Dreadnought Saves the World

4

Danny Dreadnought was not afraid of anything!

He was not afraid of heights.

He was not afraid of the dark.

And he was definitely not afraid of creepy-crawlies.

Mr and Mrs Dreadnought were very worried about him.

'It's not normal,' said Mr Dreadnought.
'It's not natural,' Mrs Dreadnought
agreed.

So they decided that Danny must
learn to be afraid.

First, they took him on the biggest, scariest roller coaster they could find and made him sit right at the front.

'W-w-were you scared, Danny?' asked
Mr Dreadnought, as he climbed
shakily off.
'I'm afraid not,' said Danny. 'Can we
go again?'

11

Next, they took him to see the crocodiles at the zoo.

'Were you scared, Danny?' asked Mrs Dreadnought, when she'd finally calmed down.

'I'm afraid not,' said Danny. 'Can we have one as a pet?'

Finally, they took him to spend a night in a haunted house.

'Were you scared, Danny?' asked Danny's parents, who had not slept a wink.

'I'm afraid not,' said Danny. 'When can we move in?'

Danny's parents tried every scary
thing they could think of . . .

. . . but Danny did not
learn to be afraid.

Until . . .

17

. . . the day the BUGULONS arrived!

The Bugulons were the scariest

creatures in the entire universe.

Everyone was afraid of them and that

was just how the Bugulons liked it, as

it made everyone's planets very easy

to invade.

So when the Bugulons' Huge Scary Spaceship appeared in the sky above Danny's school, everybody ran away screaming.

Everybody except Danny, who
wanted to take a closer look.

Danny climbed on to the school roof
and stared up at the Huge Scary
Spaceship.

'Who are you?' he shouted. 'And what are you doing here?'

'We are the Bugulons,' boomed a voice from the Huge Scary Spaceship. 'We have come to invade your planet and strike fear into your tiny Earthling minds!'

'Well, I'm Danny Dreadnought,' said
Danny, 'and *I'm afraid not*!'

The Huge Scary Spaceship hung

silently in the sky for a moment.

'Really?' said the Bugulons. 'You're not

even a teensy bit scared?'

'Not even a teensy-weensy bit,'
said Danny.

'Well, we'll see about that!' said the Bugulons and Danny felt himself being pulled upwards, high into the air, towards the Huge Scary Spaceship.

'Now are you frightened?' asked the
Bugulons.

'I'm afraid not,' said Danny. 'I'm not
scared of heights!'

Danny was sucked up through a hole into the Huge Scary Spaceship. He could hear strange click-clacking noises all around him, but there was not enough light to see what was making them.

'Now are you frightened?' hissed the Bugulons, from somewhere nearby.

'I'm afraid not,' said Danny. 'I'm not scared of the dark!'

Suddenly, the lights came on and Danny
found himself surrounded by hundreds
of Bugulons. They were rattling their
pincers and clattering their shells

and doing everything they
could to look completely terrifying!
'NOW ARE YOU SCARED?!' they
all roared.

Danny looked around and rolled his eyes.

'I'm DEFINITELY NOT afraid of creepy-crawlies!' he said, shaking his head.

The Bugulons could not hide their disappointment.

'We thought the Earthlings would be scared of us!' said one of them. 'Just like everyone else.'

'And this one's only little,' said another. 'Just think how brave the grown-ups must be!'

'We'd better put him back before any more of them arrive,' agreed a third.

So they put Danny back on the ground and flew away as fast as their Huge Scary Spaceship would carry them.

The school was empty . . .

. . . so Danny went home.

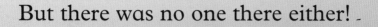

But there was no one there either! _

Mum?
Dad?

Danny couldn't believe it. His parents were ALWAYS there when he got home.

Where could they possibly be? What if they had run away like everyone else and left Danny behind?

Danny suddenly had a horrible, heavy feeling, like he was being squashed inside. His lip began to tremble and tears welled up in his eyes.

What if . . .?

Just then, his parents appeared.

They had gone out looking for Danny as soon as the Huge Scary Spaceship had arrived.

Danny's parents picked him up and hugged him tight.

'Where have you been?' they asked.

So Danny wiped away his tears and
told them.

... and then
they flew off!

'I think,' said Mr Dreadnought, when
Danny had finished, 'that we should
stop worrying about you never being
afraid.'

'If it hadn't been for that,' agreed Mrs
Dreadnought, 'we would have been
invaded by the Bugulons!'

'But I *was* afraid!' said Danny. 'I was afraid that you'd run away and left me.'

'Well that's one thing you should never be afraid of!' said Mr Dreadnought. 'No matter how scary things get, we'd never run away and leave you!' agreed Mrs Dreadnought.

'Never?' asked Danny. 'Not even if the Bugulons came back?'

Danny's parents looked at each other and grinned.

'We're afraid not!' they said.